MEZZO-SOPRANO/BEL

MUSICAL THEATRE ESS

VOLUME 1

Compiled and Edited by
Richard Walters

Published by
Hal Leonard Europe
A Music Sales / Hal Leonard Joint Venture Company
14-15 Berners Street, London W1T 3LJ, UK.

Exclusive Distributors:
Music Sales Limited
Distribution Centre, Newmarket Road
Bury St Edmunds, Suffolk IP33 3YB, UK.

Order No. HLE90004233
ISBN 978-1-61780-443-4
This book © Copyright 2012 Hal Leonard Europe

Your Guarantee of Quality
As publishers, we strive to produce every book to the highest commercial standards.
The book has been carefully designed to minimise awkward page turns and to make playing from it a real pleasure.
Throughout, the printing and binding have been planned to ensure a sturdy, attractive publication which should give years of enjoyment.
If your copy fails to meet our high standards, please inform us and we will gladly replace it.

www.musicsales.com

This publication is not authorised for sale in the
United States of America and/or Canada.

HAL LEONARD EUROPE
DISTRIBUTED BY MUSIC SALES

CONTENTS

ABOUT THE SHOWS AND SONGS

AIDA
The Past Is Another Land

Music by Elton John
Lyrics by Tim Rice
Book by Linda Woolverton, Robert Falls and David Henry Hwang
Opened in New York 23 March 2000

Aida is based on the story of the 1871 opera by Giuseppe Verdi (libretto by Antonio Ghislanzoni) about the Ethiopian princess Aida who is captured during wartime by the enemy Egyptians. Radames, an Egyptian general, and Aida fall in love **("The Past Is Another Land").** Aida is scorned by the daughter of the Egyptian King Amneris, who is also in love with Radames. Much later, Radames plans to call off his wedding to Amneris to be with Aida, but Aida convinces him to keep up appearances so she can flee from captivity with her father. Amneris overhears their exchange and realizes that their marriage plans are a sham. At their parting, Radames and Aida wonder if their love was doomed at the outset. The story ends tragically with the death of the two lovers. As of this writing in 2012 *Aida* has not had a professional production in the UK.

AVENUE Q
There's A Fine, Fine Line

Music and Lyrics by Robert Lopez and Jeff Marx
Book by Jeff Whitty
Opened in New York 31 July 2003
Opened in London 2006

Avenue Q is an ironic homage to *Sesame Street*, though the puppet characters are much more adult, dealing with topics such as loud lovemaking, closeted homosexuality, and internet porn addiction. The puppeteers are onstage, acting and singing for their characters, but there are also humans in the production. The story is of a young college graduate, Princeton, who learns how to live life and find love in New York. Along the way we meet the many tenants in his apartment building on Avenue Q. Princeton and his love interest Kate Monster hit some rocky times, and as they break up, Kate sadly muses **"There's A Fine, Fine Line"** between a lover and a friend.

BEAUTY AND THE BEAST
A Change in Me

Music by Alan Menken
Lyrics by Howard Ashman and Tim Rice
Book by Linda Woolverton
Based on the Film Released 22 November 1991, Walt Disney Pictures
Opened in New York 18 April 1994
Opened in London 29 April 1997

Disney made its Broadway debut with a big-budget adaptation of its own 1991 Oscar-nominated musical film. Like the classic fairy tale on which it is based, *Beauty And The Beast* tells the story of a witch who transforms a haughty prince into a fearsome Beast (and his servants into household objects). The spell can be broken only when the prince learns how to love, and how to inspire love. Lyricist Ashman died in 1991 before the film was released. The stage score includes several songs written for the film but not used, plus five new songs with lyrics by veteran Tim Rice. Headstrong young woman Belle discovers the Beast's castle after her father is captured and held prisoner there. She bravely offers to exchange herself for her father and soon finds herself adopted by the various living clocks, teapots, candlesticks, and cutlery who strive to play matchmaker of their beastly boss and the eligible but understandably resistant maiden. In **"A Change In Me,"** Belle realizes that her feelings for the increasingly gentlemanly Beast are beginning to soften. The song was added to the show mid-run when pop diva Toni Braxton played Belle.

CABARET
Maybe This Time

Music by John Kander
Lyrics by Fred Ebb
Book by Joe Masteroff
Opened in New York 20 November 1966
Opened in London 28 February 1968

This moody musical captures the morally corrupt world of Berlin's demimonde just as the Nazis were coming to power. American writer Cliff Bradshaw moves in with Sally Bowles, the hedonistic British singer at a seedy nightclub. Soon, he comes to see all of Germany through the dark lens of that increasingly menacing cabaret, which is ruled over by a ghostly Emcee. The first London production starred Judi Dench as Sally. A revival played in London in 1986, and in New York in 1987. The 1972 film used a different story from the original stage show. Two songs were added to the film version to build up the role of Sally for star Liza Minnelli. She gives a Dietrich-like come-on to men everywhere in "Mein Herr," and lets her cynicism slip for just a moment in the hopeful ballad **"Maybe This Time."** These songs and other aspects of the film were incorporated in the 1993 London revival, directed by Sam Mendes. The same production was adapted for Broadway for a 1998 opening. A further revival opened in London in 2006.

CHESS
Heaven Help My Heart

Music by Benny Andersson and Björn Ulvaeus
Lyrics by Tim Rice
Book by Richard Nelson, based on an idea by Tim Rice
Opened in London 14 May 1986
Opened in New York 28 April 1988

There had been musicals about the cold war (*Leave It To Me!, Silk Stockings*), but *Chess* was the first to treat the conflict seriously, using an international chess match as a metaphor. The idea originated with Tim Rice who first tried to interest his former partner, Andrew Lloyd Webber, in the project. When that failed, he approached Andersson and Ulvaeus, writers and singers with the Swedish pop group ABBA. Like *Jesus Christ Superstar* and *Evita*, *Chess* originated as a successful concept album, released in 1984, before it became a stage musical. The London production was a high-tech spectacle, rock opera-type presentation. The libretto was revised for New York, and a different production approach was tried. It is ironic that the musical opened on Broadway at the tail end of the Cold War era, which may have made the subject matter seem less than current. The story is a romantic triangle with a Bobby Fischer-type American chess champion, a Russian opponent who defects to the West, and the Hungarian-born American, Florence, who transfers her affections from the American to the Russian without bringing happiness to anyone. Realizing early on the futility of her love for the Russian, Florence sings of her predicament in the ballad **"Heaven Help My Heart."**

Although the show was poorly received in the US, and there have been no full revivals in London or New York, the score retains a strong following. A noteworthy 2008 concert performance was presented at Royal Albert Hall, and subsequently released on DVD. Tim Rice called this the "official version" of the show, after many years of changes.

COMPANY
Another Hundred People

Music and Lyrics by Stephen Sondheim
Book by George Furth
Opened in New York 26 April 1970
Opened in London 18 January, 1972

Company was the first of the Sondheim musicals to have been directed by Harold Prince, and more than any other musical reflects urban America in the 1970s. The show is a plotless evening about five affluent couples living in a Manhattan apartment building and their excessively protective feeling about a charming, but somewhat indifferent bachelor named Bobby. At his 35th birthday, they want to fix him up and see him married. In the end, he is ready for intimacy in a committed relationship, despite all the problems he sees in his friends' marriages. The songs are often very sophisticated, expressing the ambivalent or caustic attitudes of fashionable New Yorkers. Marta, one of Bobby's girlfriends, sings **"Another Hundred People,"** about urban alienation of individuals, as Bobby is seen on dates with various women. The authors revised the original libretto in the late 1980s. A revival opened in both London and New York in 1995, each by a different director. A unique revival concept opened on Broadway in 2006, with the cast playing instruments in a greatly reduced orchestration.

DREAMGIRLS
And I Am Telling You I'm Not Going
I Am Changing

Music by Henry Krieger
Lyrics and Book by Tom Eyen
Opened in New York 20 December 1981

With *Dreamgirls*, Michael Bennett returned to the heartbreak world of show business that he had explored in *A Chorus Line* to create another high-voltage concept musical. Tom Eyen's tough-tender book about the corruption of innocence of a singing group of the 1960s, The Dreams, was vaguely and loosely a fictionalized Motown story about the Supremes. Powerhouse voice Effie Melody White, is dropped for the more commercial and simpler lead voice in the group, Deena. There are romantic upsets as well. The trio rises to stardom, and Effie struggles but finally finds a career of her own. The most famous song from the show comes near the end of Act I. **"And I Am Telling You I'm Not Going"** is sung by Effie to Curtis, manager of the group and her boyfriend, after he has fired her and replaced her with another singer. What Curtis does not know is that Effie has missed a few performances because she is having a rough start to a pregnancy with his child. Despite Effie's plea, she does leave the group and moves back home to Chicago. Five difficult years later, now a single mother with a daughter, Effie finally lets go of her anger and begins to find a new attitude and act in **"I Am Changing."** A film version of the show was released in 2006, starring Jennifer Hudson and Beyoncé Knowles. To this author's knowledge, at the time of this writing (2012) *Dreamgirls* has never played in a professional London production.

EVITA
Don't Cry For Me Argentina

Music by Andrew Lloyd Webber
Lyrics and Book by Tim Rice
Opened in London 23 June 1978
Opened in New York 25 September 1979

The rock musical began as a concept album, released in 1976, followed by a successful 1978 stage premiere in London. *Evita* was practically a pre-sold hit when it began its run on Broadway in 1979. Based on events in the life of Argentina's strong-willed leader, Eva Peron, the musical traced her rise from struggling actress to wife of Dictator Juan Peron, and virtual co-ruler of the country. Though the plot was told entirely through song and had originally been conceived as a project for recording, the razzle-dazzle staging of Harold Prince turned Evita into an exciting theatrical concept that has been hailed throughout the world. Of no little help, of course, has been the universal popularity of the haunting melody **"Don't Cry For Me Argentina,"** Eva's address to her public. A film version was released in 1996, starring Madonna as Eva and Antonio Banderas as Che. The musical was revived in the West End in 2006; a Broadway revival opened in 2012.

FLOWER DRUM SONG
I Enjoy Being A Girl

Music by Richard Rodgers
Lyrics by Oscar Hammerstein II
Book by Oscar Hammerstein II and Joseph Fields
Opened in New York 1 December 1958
Opened in London 24 March 1960

It was librettist Joseph Fields who first secured the rights to C.Y. Lee's novel and then approached Rodgers and Hammerstein to join him as collaborators. To dramatize the conflict between the traditional older Chinese-Americans living in San Francisco and their thoroughly Americanized offspring, the musical tells the story of Mei Li, a timid "picture bride" from China, who arrives to fulfill her contract to marry nightclub owner Sammy Fong. Sammy, however, prefers dancer Linda Low. The problem is resolved when Sammy's friend Wang Ta discovers that Mei Li really is the bride for him. Early in the show, Linda sings a bouncy tribute to the life of lipstick, lace, and flowers in **"I Enjoy Being A Girl."** A film version of the musical was released in 1961. A revised libretto by playwright David Henry Hwang was used in the Broadway revival of 2002.

FOLLIES
Losing My Mind

Music and Lyrics by Stephen Sondheim
Book by James Goldman
Opened in New York 4 April 1971
Opened in London 21 July 1987

Taking place at a 1971 reunion of former Ziegfeld Follies-type showgirls of the 1930s at the soon to be demolished Weismann Theatre, the musical deals with the reality of life as contrasted with the unreality of the theatre. It explores this theme through the lives of two couples, the upper class, unhappy Phyllis and Benjamin Stone, and the middle-class, unhappy Sally and Buddy Plummer. *Follies* also depicts these four as they were in their pre-marital youth. Because the plotless show is about the past, and often in flashback, using rather cinematic devices, Sondheim purposefully stylized some of songs in the score to evoke some of the theatre's great composers and lyricists of the 1930s. In Act II, a pastiche section puts the principal characters through a stylized follies, while revealing their inner conflicts and feelings. Sally sings **"Losing My Mind."** In his book *Finishing The Hat* Sondheim says of the song, "Musically, this was less an homage to, than a theft of, Gershwin's 'The Man I Love,' complete with near-stenciled rhythms and harmonies. But it had a difference: a lyric written not in the style of his brother, but of Dorothy Fields." The revised version of the show presented in London in 1987, replaced some songs with new numbers. *Follies* was given two concert performances in 1985 at Avery Fisher Hall in New York with an all star cast, resulting in the most revered recording of the show. Barbara Cook performed the role of Sally in that concert and recording. An acclaimed revival of the musical opened on Broadway in 2011.

GODSPELL
Turn Back, O Man

Music and Lyrics by Stephen Schwartz
Book by John-Michael Tebelak
Opened in New York 5 May 1971
Opened in London 17 November 1971

With its rock-flavored score, *Godspell* is a flower-child view of the Gospel of St. Matthew. Jesus, depicted as a clown-faced innocent with a Superman "S" on his shirt, leads a band of followers in dramatized parables, including the Prodigal Son, the Good Samaritan, the Pharisees, and the Tax Collector. The funky **"Turn Back, O Man"** was sung by the troupe's scarlet woman, who bumped her way up and down the aisles of the theatre during her rendition, á la Mae West. The 1971 London production featured David Hemmings, Jeremy Irons, Johanna Cassidy and Marti Webb. A film version was released in 1973.

GUYS AND DOLLS
Adelaide's Lament

Music and Lyrics by Frank Loesser
Book by Abe Burrows and Jo Swerling
Opened in New York 24 November 1950
Opened in London 28 May 1953

Populated by the hard-shelled but soft-centered characters who inhabit the world of writer Damon Runyon, this "Musical Fable of Broadway" tells the tale of how Miss Sarah Brown of the Save-a-Soul Mission saves the souls of assorted Times Square riff-raff while losing her heart to the smooth-talking gambler, Sky Masterson. A more comic romance involves Nathan Detroit, who runs the "oldest established permanent floating game of craps in New York," and Miss Adelaide, the star of the Hot Box nightclub, to whom he has been engaged for fourteen years, which explains her famous song, **"Adelaide's Lament."** The gamblers resist Sarah's evangelism, but she wins Sky's heart, and he leaves his life of crime behind for her. At the end of the show Adelaide finally may be heading to the altar with Nathan. *Guys And Dolls* is considered one of the best musical comedies of the 20th century. For many years Laurence Olivier wanted to play the character Nathan Detroit, but that production was never mounted. An all black cast played in a Broadway revival of 1976. A major revival opened in London in 1982 at the National Theatre. A 1992 Broadway revival was an enormous success. Further revivals played in the West End in 1996 and 2005. The 1955 film version starred Frank Sinatra as Nathan Detroit, Marlon Brando as Sky Masterson, Jean Simmons as Sarah, and Vivian Blaine (the only remnant of the Broadway cast) as Adelaide.

HAIRSPRAY
I Can Hear The Bells

Music by Marc Shaiman
Lyrics by Scott Wittman and Marc Shaiman
Book by Mark O'Donnell and Thomas Meehan
Opened in New York 15 August 2002
Opened in London 11 October 2007

Film composer Marc Shaiman helped turn John Waters' campy 1988 movie *Hairspray* into perfect fodder for a new Broadway musical—teenage angst, racial integration, a lot of dancing, and a whole lot of hair. Taking place in Baltimore, plump heroine Tracy Turnblad dreams of dancing on the Corny Collins TV show, but is upstaged by the prettier, but less talented, current "it-girl" Amber Von Tussle. Tracy envisions good things for herself, as she knows she can take down Amber in **"I Can Hear The Bells."** Tracy eventually dances her way onto the Corny Collins TV show and gains acceptance for all teens of every size, shape, and color.

INTO THE WOODS
I Know Things Now

Music and Lyrics by Stephen Sondheim
Book by James Lapine
Opened in New York 5 November 1987
Opened in London 25 September 1990

Into the Woods brought together for the second time the Pulitzer Prize winning team of Lapine and Sondheim. After their first collaboration, *Sunday In The Park With George*, this time they turned to children's fairy tales as their subject. The book of *Into The Woods* often focuses on the darker, grotesque aspects of these stories, but by highlighting them, it touches on themes of interpersonal relationships, death, and what we pass onto our children. Act I begins with the familiar "once upon a time" stories, and masterfully interweaves the plots of Snow White, Little Red Ridinghood, Cinderella, Jack and the Beanstalk, a Baker and his Wife, and others. Act II concerns what happens after "happily ever after," as reality sets in, and the fairy tales plots dissolve into the more human stories. Little Red Ridinghood sings the moral of her tale in **"I Know Things Now"** after disobeying her mother and ending up lunch to a hungry wolf. Revivals played in London in 1998, 2007, and in 2010 at the Regent's Park Open Air Theatre.

JEKYLL & HYDE
Someone Like You

Music by Frank Wildhorn
Lyrics and Book by Leslie Bricusse
Opened in New York 28 April 28 1997

The musical is based on Robert Louis Stevenson's 1886 novella *Strange Case Of Dr. Jekyll And Mr. Hyde*. As in the book, a well-meaning scientist, Dr. Henry Jekyll, invents a potion that separates the noble side of man's nature from the evil, bestial side. Using himself as guinea pig, Jekyll soon finds he has unleashed an uncontrollable monster, Mr. Hyde, who cuts a murderous swath through London. Two women in his life help emphasize this difference: Jekyll's sweet innocent fiancée, Emma; and Hyde's scarlet-woman love, Lucy. Injured by a rough customer, Lucy finds herself being treated by the gentle Dr. Jekyll, and she fantasizes about a relationship with him in **"Someone Like You."** A UK tour was launched in 2004. Another UK tour began in 2011.

THE LAST FIVE YEARS
Still Hurting

Music by Jason Robert Brown
Lyrics and Book by Jason Robert Brown
Opened in New York 3 March 2002
Opened in London 28 September 2010

The Off-Broadway musical *The Last Five Years* paired writer Jason Robert Brown and director Daisy Prince (daughter of Harold) together again after their collaboration on the revue *Songs For A New World*. This two-person show chronicles the beginning, middle and deterioration of a relationship between a successful writer and a struggling actress. The show's form is unique. Cathy starts at the end of the relationship, and tells her story backwards, while Jamie starts at the beginning. The only point of intersection is the middle at their engagement. The relationship has taken its toll on Cathy; she is **"Still Hurting"** after the break-up (the show's opening song), wondering about the love and the lies that Jamie gave her.

THE LITTLE MERMAID
Part Of Your World

Music by Alan Menken
Lyrics by Howard Ashman; additional Broadway lyrics by Glenn Slater
Book by Doug Wright
Based on the film released 17 November 1989, Walt Disney Pictures
Opened in New York 10 January 2008

Based on the Hans Christian Andersen tale, *The Little Mermaid* marked the Disney studio's triumphant return to the animated screen musical. Ariel, a young sea-dwelling mermaid, longs to be human. She falls in love with the human prince and, aided by some magic, gets her wish. **"Part Of Your World"** is sung by Ariel as she observes human life from the water she cannot leave. The musical was adapted and expanded for the Broadway stage, with added songs. As of this writing (2012), the musical has not played in the West End.

A LITTLE NIGHT MUSIC
Send In The Clowns

Music and Lyrics by Stephen Sondheim
Book by Hugh Wheeler
Opened in New York 25 February 1973
Opened in London 15 April 1975

Based on Ingmar Bergman's 1955 film, *Smiles Of A Summer Night, A Little Night Music* could claim two musical distinctions: the entire Stephen Sondheim score was composed in time signatures of 3 (or multiples thereof) and it contained, in **"Send In The Clowns,"** the biggest song hit that Sondheim ever wrote. The musical is about a group of well-to-do Swedes at the turn of the last century, among them a lawyer, Fredrik Egerman; his virginal child bride, Anne; his former mistress, the actress Désirée Armfeldt; Désirée's current lover, the aristocratic Count Carl-Magnus Malcolm; and the count's suicidal wife, Charlotte. All find themselves invited for a weekend at the country house of Désirée's mother, a former concubine of European nobility. After years of touring and not knowing what she wanted, Désirée is now sure she wants Fredrik. In a scene between Désirée and Fredrik she sings to him **"Send In The Clowns"** about their ironic predicament of bad timing in their relationship. Because of Désirée's profession as an actress, the lyrics of the song use theatrical terms as metaphors. After many emotional cross-signals, eventually, the proper partners are sorted out. Désirée and Frederik end up together, as do Anne and Henrik, Fredrik's teenage son. A West End revival opened in 1989. A Royal National Theatre production, starring Judi Dench as Désirée, opened in 1995. A Menier Chocolate Factory revival, directed by Trevor Nunn, opened in London in 2007; this same production opened on Broadway in 2009, starring Catherine Zeta-Jones and Angela Lansbury. Those stars were succeeded on Broadway by Bernadette Peters and Elaine Stritch. A film version, with the location moved from Sweden to Austria, was released in 1977.

MAMMA MIA!
The Winner Takes It All

Music and Lyrics by Benny Andersson and Björn Ulvaeus
Book by Catherine Johnson
Opened in London 6 April 1999
Opened in New York 18 October 2001

Mamma Mia! is a "jukebox musical" culled from the catalogue of Swedish pop group ABBA. Over 20 songs are used in the show, more or less in their original form, woven into a libretto created for the stage production. It takes place on a fictional Greek Island where Donna Sheridan runs a small tavern. Her daughter, Sophie, has always wanted to know the identity of her father, but Donna has refused to reveal the information. Sophie sneaks a read of Donna's old diaries, and invites three men from the past, one of whom she believes is possibly her father, to her upcoming wedding. Donna realizes that she still loves one of the men, Sam, though she doesn't want to admit it. It turns out that long ago Sam was having an affair with Donna while being engaged to another woman, and Donna is still angry about it. She sings **"The Winner Takes It All"** remembering the old predicament and her feelings. It's never clear who Sophie's father really is, but she comes to love all three men. She calls her wedding off, but Donna connects with her old beau Sam, who is now single and available. The wedding plans stay in place, but Donna and Sam get married instead. The show is a good time for audiences familiar with the great pop songs of the score. The 2008 film version starred Meryl Streep as Donna.

LES MISÉRABLES
I Dreamed A Dream

Music by Claude-Michel Schönberg
Lyrics by Herbert Kretzmer and Alain Boublil
Original French Text by Alain Boublil and Jean-Marc Natel
Opened in Paris September 1980
Expanded and rewritten English version opened in London 8 October 1985
Opened in New York 12 March 1987

This pop-opera epic was one of the defining musicals of the 1980s and continues its appeal, distilling the drama from the 1200 page Victor Hugo novel of social injustice and the plight of the downtrodden (the "miserable ones" of the title). The original Parisian version contained only a few songs; many more were added when the show opened in London. Thus, most of the show's songs were originally performed in English. The dense plot is too rich to encapsulate, but centers on Jean Valjean, a prisoner sentenced to years of hard labor for stealing a loaf of bread for his starving family. He escapes and tries to start a new life, but soon finds himself hunted by the relentless Javert. The pursuit continues for years, across a tapestry of 19th century France that includes an armed uprising against the government, in which Valjean takes a heroic part. Along the way he tries to help the destitute Fantine. Early in the show she sings **"I Dreamed A Dream"** as she lies ill and dying.

OKLAHOMA!
I Cain't Say No

Music by Richard Rodgers
Lyrics and Book by Oscar Hammerstein II
Opened in New York 31 March 1943
Opened in London 30 August 1947

Oklahoma!, based on the play *Green Grow the Lilacs* by Lynn Riggs, is set in the summer of 1907 just prior to the admission of the Indian Territory Oklahoma as a state.

Ado Annie Carnes is an unsophisticated, high-spirited ranch girl whose pa has told Will Parker that if he comes up with $50 he can marry her. Will wins $50 in a rodeo in Kansas City, but while he's away Ado Annie agrees to go to the box social with peddler Ali Hakim. Attracted to both men, she sings of her predicament in **"I Cain't Say No."** With its Broadway run of five years, nine months, *Oklahoma!* established a long-run record that it held for 15 years, until being overtaken by *My Fair Lady*. *Oklahoma!* was among the first batch of new Broadway musicals to open in London after the end of World War II, achieving great success with Howard Keel as Curly. A prominent London production directed by Trevor Nunn opened in 1998 at the National Theatre, with Hugh Jackman as Curly. This production was adapted for a 2002 Broadway revival with a different cast. The film version was released in 1955.

THE PRODUCERS
When You Got It, Flaunt It

Music and Lyrics by Mel Brooks
Book by Mel Brooks and Thomas Meehan
Opened in New York 19 April 2001
Opened in London 9 November 2004

Mel Brooks swept critics and audiences off their feet in New York with this show, adapted from his 1968 movie *The Producers*. A couple songs from the movie were incorporated into the otherwise new stage score. The story concerns washed-up Broadway producer Max Bialystock and his nerdy accountant Leo Bloom, who has dreams of being a producer himself. During an audit of Max's books, Leo offhandedly remarks that one could make more money producing a flop than a hit. The two eventually produce the show *Springtime for Hitler*, which seems on paper like it will be the biggest flop ever. It's a surprise hit and Bialystock and Bloom are in trouble. All ends well, after a brief prison detour. Svelte, sexy Swede Ulla comes to the offices of Bialystock and Bloom to audition (she is hired as secretary), her only talent being **"When You Got It, Flaunt It."** The original cast included Broadway stars Nathan Lane and Matthew Broderick. The director and most of the lead actors from Broadway were in the 2005 movie musical.

RENT
Without You

Music, Lyrics and Book by Jonathan Larson
Opened in New York 29 February 1996
Opened in London 21 April 1998

Jonathan Larson's musical relocates the story of Puccini's opera *La Bohème* to the 1990s in New York's East Village. Among other stories and characters, Roger Davis is an ex-junkie HIV-positive songwriter/musician whose past girlfriend, a drug addict, died of AIDS. He meets Mimi Marquez, a heroin addict, and there is an obvious spark of attraction between them. He is initially terrified of getting involved with her, but after he finds out that she is HIV-positive as well, they begin a romance. They live together for a time, but have a tempestuous relationship. Roger is extremely jealous and leaves her. Mimi contemplates being alone in **"Without You."** Months later friends bring a desperately ill Mimi back to Roger, and she dies. The compelling alternative-rock score has a gritty realism, a theatrical reflection of grunge rock of the period. A parable of hope, love and loyalty, Rent received great acclaim, winning the Pulitzer Prize for Drama, a Tony Award for Best Musical, and many other awards. Though it initially opened Off-Broadway in the New York Theatre Workshop, it soon transferred to a Broadway theatre that was redesigned to capture its East Village atmosphere. Bound up with the show's message of the preciousness of life is the tragic real-life story of its composer/librettist Jonathan Larson, who died suddenly of an aortic dissection the night of the final dress rehearsal before the first Off-Broadway preview performance. A 2005 film version featured most of the original Broadway cast.

SONGS FOR A NEW WORLD
Stars And The Moon

Music and Lyrics by Jason Robert Brown
Opened in New York 26 October 1995

In 1994, Daisy Prince, daughter of Broadway legend Harold Prince, went to hear a 24-year-old Greenwich Village coffeehouse pianist named Jason Robert Brown play some of his original songs. When she heard he was working on a concert evening of songs that played like offbeat short stories, a collaboration and a friendship began. Titled *Songs For A New World*, the piece was developed at a summer festival Livent Inc. sponsored in Toronto, and the piece made its Off-Broadway bow in October 1995. Musically distinctive and precocious, the songs look at contemporary life from highly unusual angles. In **"Stars And The Moon,"** a woman regrets that she's been offered those two commodities by a series of idealistic, worshipping men, but she's always turned them down in favor of safer, more earthly pleasures. Brown's next project, *Parade*, was directed by Prince appearing on Broadway in 1998, and won him the 1999 Tony Award for Best Score.

SOUTH PACIFIC
Honey Bun

Music by Richard Rodgers
Lyrics by Oscar Hammerstein II
Book by Oscar Hammerstein II and Joshua Logan
Opened in New York 7 April 1949
Opened in London 1 November 1951

On a U.S. Naval base in the south Pacific during World War II, an unlikely romance develops between Nellie Forbush, a naïve navy nurse from Little Rock, and Emile de Becque, a sophisticated French planter living on the island. The musical is based on two short stories from *Tales Of The South Pacific* by James Michener. For a follies revue show put on for the troops, Nellie gets into the spirit, dresses as a male sailor, and sings the raucous number **"Honey Bun"** to Luther Billis who is dressed as a hula-skirted native girl. Nellie, in love with de Becque, overcomes her prejudice at his children born of a now dead Polynesian wife. The musical was revived in London in 1988, and in 2001 in a production directed by Trevor Nunn. A prominent and successful Broadway revival opened in 2008.

SWEET CHARITY
If My Friends Could See Me Now

Music by Cy Coleman
Lyrics by Dorothy Fields
Book by Neil Simon
Opened in New York 29 January 1966
Opened in London October 1967

Bob Fosse initiated the project, based on the Federico Fellini 1957 film *Le Notti Di Cabiria*. Originally intended as the first half of a double bill of one-act musicals, *Sweet Charity* was fleshed out to two acts when Neil Simon took over the writing. Charity Hope Valentine is a New York dance hall hostess who knows there's gotta be something better than working at the Fandango Ballroom. She is big-hearted and open to anything that comes her way. As she walks past the Pompeii Club an Italian movie star, Vittorio Vidal, comes out while chasing his mistress, who has stormed out. When the mistress refuses to return to the club with him, he instead invites Charity, who just happens to be there. She accepts, but faints due to hunger while dancing with him. He takes her back to his apartment. Charity suddenly feels fine once there and can't believe her luck at being in such luxurious surroundings in the home of a celebrity, singing **"If My Friends Could See Me Now."** Later she becomes entangled with another man, Oscar. *Sweet Charity* has been revived twice to date on Broadway, in 1986 and 2007. London revivals opened in 1998, and more successfully in 2009. A film version, directed by Bob Fosse and starring Shirley MacLaine, was released in 1969. John McMartin repeated his stage role as Oscar in the movie.

THOROUGHLY MODERN MILLIE
Gimme Gimme

Music by Jeanine Tesori
Lyrics by Dick Scanlan
Book by Dick Scanlan and Richard Morris
Opened in New York 18 April 2002
Opened in London 21 October 2003

Based on the 1967 movie starring Julie Andrews, *Thoroughly Modern Millie* is a new musical, retaining only three of the songs from the movie (including the title song), with a score by Jeanine Tesori. It chronicles the life of Millie, a transplanted Kansas girl trying to make it big in New York in the flapper days of the 1920s. She stays at the Hotel Priscilla, along with other young starlets, which is managed by the sinister Mrs. Meers, who actually is running a white slave trade on the side. The madcap plot has many twists and turns, and shows a cheery slice of life in New York during the Jazz age. Millie decides in the end that it is only love she is interested in. She belts this sentiment high and loud in **"Gimme Gimme."**

WICKED
Defying Gravity

Music and Lyrics by Stephen Schwartz
Book by Winnie Holzman,
   based on the novel *Wicked: The Life And Times Of The Wicked Witch Of The West* by Gregory Maguire
Opened in New York 30 October 2003
Opened in London 27 September 2006

Stephen Schwartz's return to Broadway came with the hit musical *Wicked*. Based on Gregory Maguire's 1995 book, the musical chronicles the backstory of the Wicked Witch of the West, Elphaba, and Good Witch of the North, Glinda (Galinda), before their story threads are picked up in L. Frank Baum's *The Wonderful Wizard Of Oz*. As the musical begins, the citizens of Oz celebrate the death of the Wicked Witch of the West, led by Glinda. A flashback begins that tells the story of the complex relationship between the two witches. Glinda and Elphaba form a friendship in secret and unite against the duplicitous Wizard. After being labeled "wicked" Elphaba casts a spell on a broomstick to make it fly, and she flies off, vowing to fight the Wizard in the song **"Defying Gravity,"** which ends Act I.

THE WILD PARTY
How Did We Come To This?

Music, Lyrics and Book by Andrew Lippa
Opened in New York 24 February 2000

Two productions of *The Wild Party* hit New York in 2000, the unsuccessful Broadway show by Michael John LaChiusa, and the Off-Broadway, and now more popular Andrew Lippa musical. Both were based on the scandalous 1928 poem by The New Yorker editor Joseph Moncure March. This jazz age drama, depicting a night of decadence and debauchery at a party thrown by lusty showgirl Queenie and her abusive lover, vaudeville clown Burrs, was inspiration for Lippa's accomplished score. Kate, a semi-reformed hooker, arrives with her squeeze, Mr. Black. After the wanton night of excessive partying and drama, Queenie surveys the scene in **"How Did We Come To This?"** to end the show

THE PAST IS ANOTHER LAND

from Elton John and Tim Rice's *Aida*

Music by ELTON JOHN
Lyrics by TIM RICE

Gently, moderately

A CHANGE IN ME

from Walt Disney's *Beauty And The Beast: The Broadway Musical*

Words by TIM RICE
Music by ALAN MENKEN

This song has been transposed up an augmented second from the original key.

No change of heart, a change in me. _____

THERE'S A FINE, FINE LINE
from the Broadway Musical *Avenue Q*

Music and Lyrics by ROBERT LOPEZ
and JEFF MARX

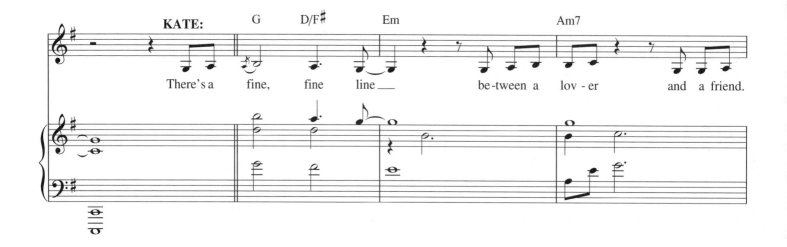

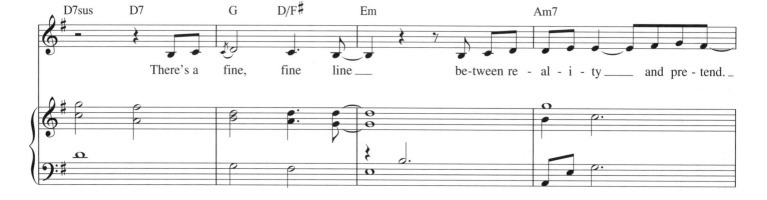

MAYBE THIS TIME
from the Musical *Cabaret*

Words by FRED EBB
Music by JOHN KANDER

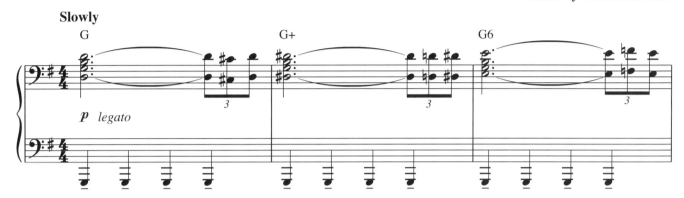

May-be this time_ I'll be luck-y.__ May-be this time_ he'll

stay. May-be this time,_ for the first time,_ love won't hur-ry a-

In the 1998 Broadway Revival this final section was performed in an understated, soft way.

HEAVEN HELP MY HEART
from *Chess*

Words and Music by BENNY ANDERSSON,
TIM RICE and BJÖRN ULVAEUS

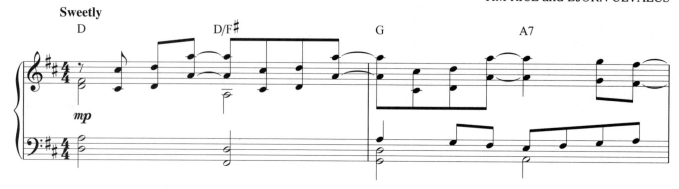

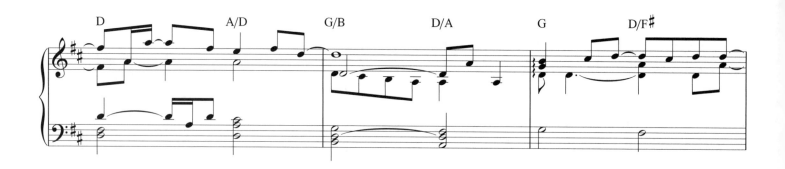

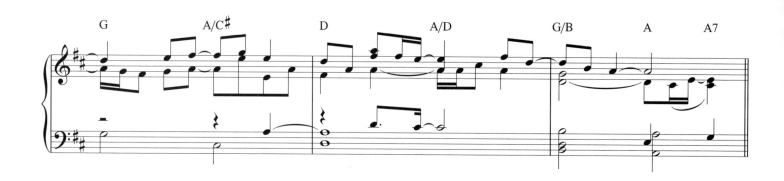

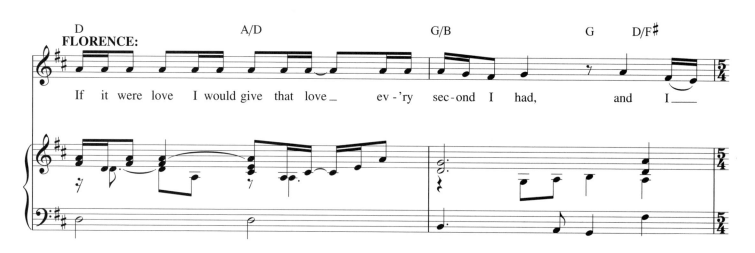

FLORENCE:

If it were love I would give that love __ ev-'ry sec-ond I had, and I__

ANOTHER HUNDRED PEOPLE
from *Company*

Music and Lyrics by
STEPHEN SONDHEIM

oth - er hun-dred peo-ple who got off of the plane _ And are look-ing at us _ Who got

off of the train _ And the plane and the bus _ May - be yes-ter-day. _____

It's a ci - ty of strang - ers, _____

Some come to work, some _ to play. _____ A ci - ty of strang - ers, ____

dust - y trees with the bat-tered barks, ___ And they

walk to-geth - er past the post - ered walls with the crude re - marks. ___

And they

meet at par - ties through the friends of friends who they nev-er know. ___

And an-

oth-er hun-dred peo-ple just got off of the train.

dim. poco a poco

An -

And an - oth-er hun-dred peo-ple just got off of the train _ And an-

*This repeat is omitted on the recording.

oth-er hun-dred peo-ple just got off of the train __ And an-oth-er hun-dred peo-ple just got

off of the train! _____

AND I AM TELLING YOU
I'M NOT GOING
from *Dreamgirls*

Music by HENRY KRIEGER
Lyric by TOM EYEN

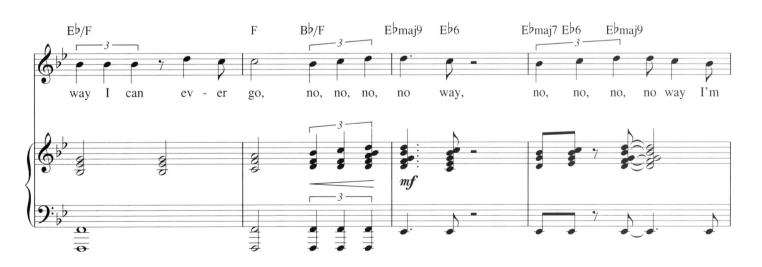

52

I AM CHANGING

from *Dreamgirls*

Music by HENRY KRIEGER
Lyric by TOM EYEN

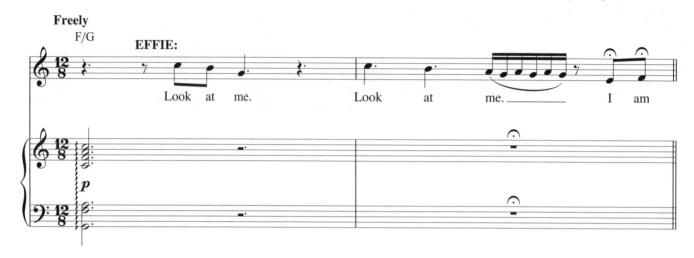

DON'T CRY FOR ME ARGENTINA

from *Evita*

Words by TIM RICE
Music by ANDREW LLOYD WEBBER

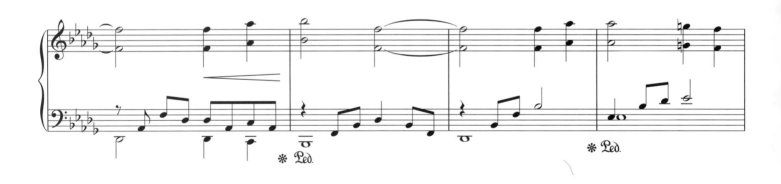

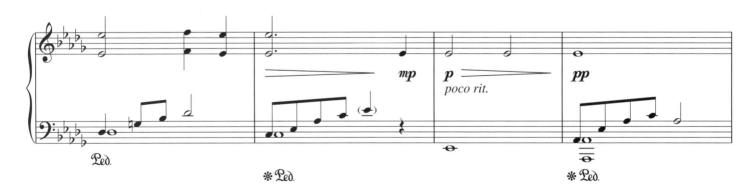

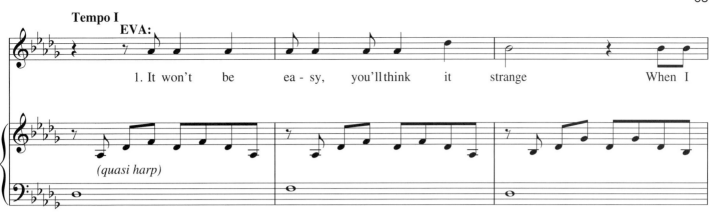

nines at six - es and sev - ens with you.

2. I had to let it hap - pen, I had to change; Could - n't

stay all my life down at heel: Look - ing out of the win - dow, stay ing

out of the sun. So I chose free - dom Run - ning a - round try - ing

ev - 'ry - thing new, but noth - ing im - pressed me at all, I

Slow Tango feel

nev - er ex - pect - ed it to. Don't cry for me Ar - gen -

ti - na _____ the truth is I nev - er left you: All through my

wild days, my mad ex - ist - ence, I kept my pro - mise, Don't keep your

all you have to do is look at me to know that ev - 'ry word is true.

Grandioso

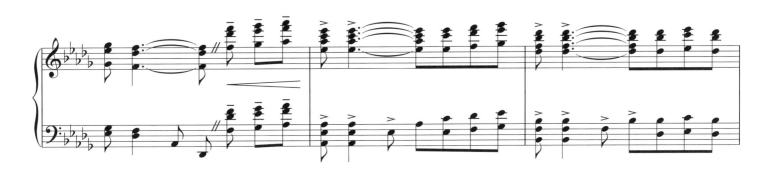

I ENJOY BEING A GIRL
from *Flower Drum Song*

Lyrics by OSCAR HAMMERSTEIN II
Music by RICHARD RODGERS

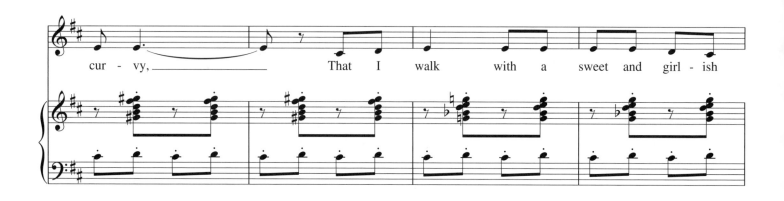

swerv - y. _____ I a - dore be - ing dressed in some-thing fril - ly _____ When my

date comes to get me at my place. Out I go with my Joe or John or Bil - ly, _____ Like a

fil - ly who is read - y for the race! _____ When

Brightly

I have a brand new hair - do _____ With my

teeth are - n't teeth but pearl, _____ I

just lap it up like hon - ey, _____ I en -

joy be - ing a girl. _____ I

flip when a fel - low sends me flow - ers, _____ I

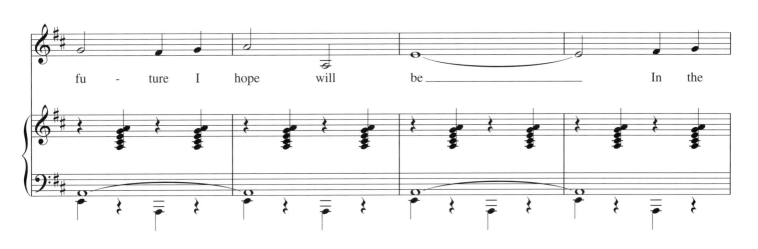

fu - ture I hope will be _____ In the

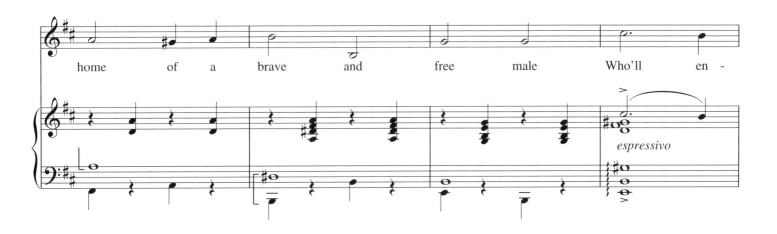

home of a brave and free male Who'll en -

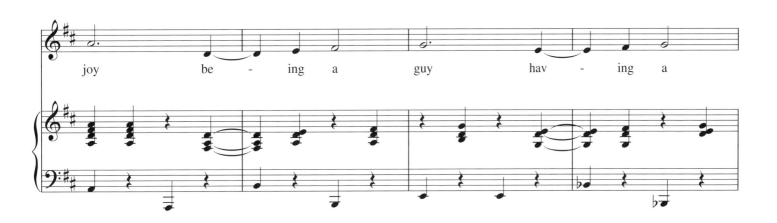

joy be - ing a guy hav - ing a

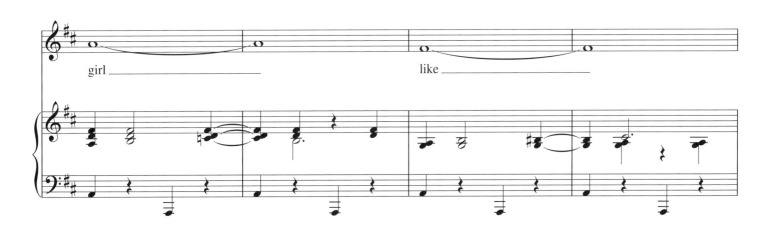

girl _____ like _____

me. _____ When

men say I'm sweet as can - dy, _____ As a -

round in a dance we whirl, _____ It

goes to my head like bran - dy, _____ I en -

joy be - ing a girl. _____ When some - one with eyes that smoul - der _____ says he loves ev - 'ry silk - en curl_____ That falls on my iv' - ry shoul - der, _____ I en - joy be - ing a girl. _____

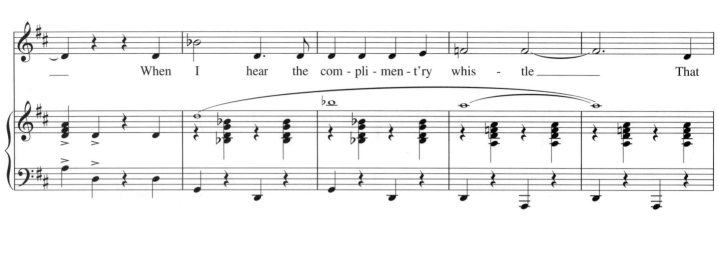

When I hear the com-pli-men-t'ry whis - tle_____ That

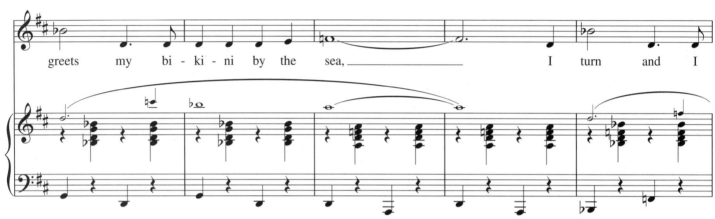

greets my bi-ki-ni by the sea,_____ I turn and I

glow-er and I bris - tle,_____ But I'm hap-py to know the whis-tle's meant for

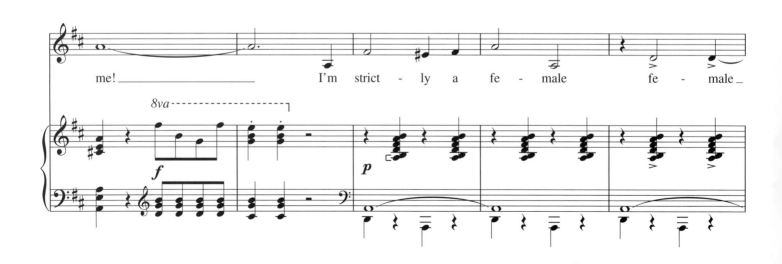

me!_____ I'm strict - ly a fe - male fe-male_____

TURN BACK, O MAN

from the Musical *Godspell*

Words and Music by
STEPHEN SCHWARTZ

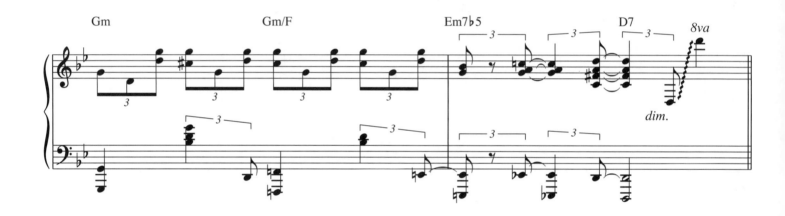

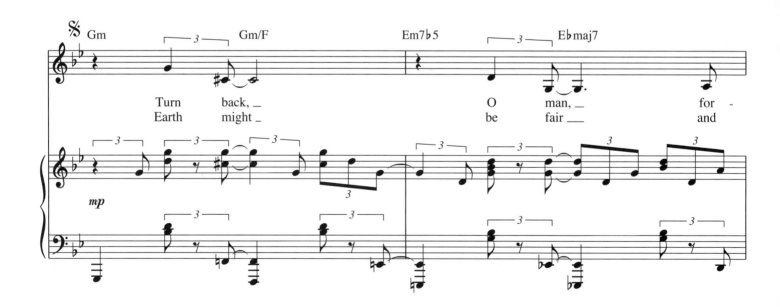

*The ad libs. (in parentheses) are merely suggestions, not necessarily the lines you will want to use.
 Ad libs., when possible, should be based on the actual audience members (for instance: "Hiya, Curly" to a bald man, etc.)

swear thy _ fool - ish _ ways. _ *Spoken: See ya' later—I'm going to the front of the the-a-ter.*

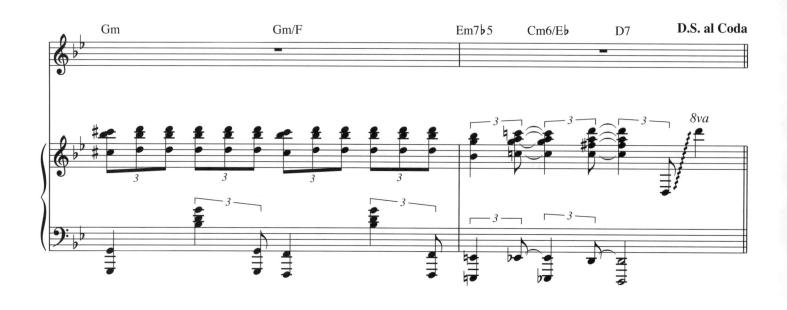

D.S. al Coda

CODA

Turn back, _ O _ man, _

LOSING MY MIND
from *Follies*

Music and Lyrics by
STEPHEN SONDHEIM

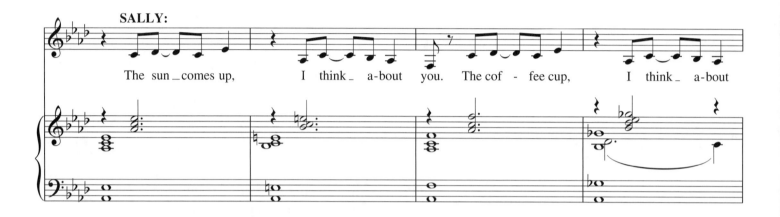

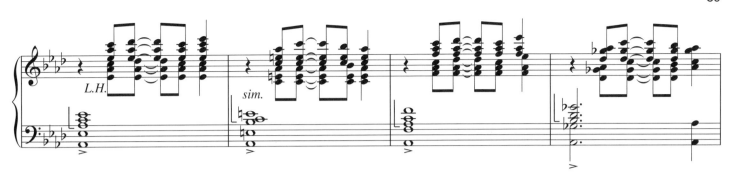

Does no — one know? It's like I'm los-ing my mind.

Faster

All af-ter-noon, do-ing ev-'ry lit-tle chore, The thought of you stays

(colla voce)

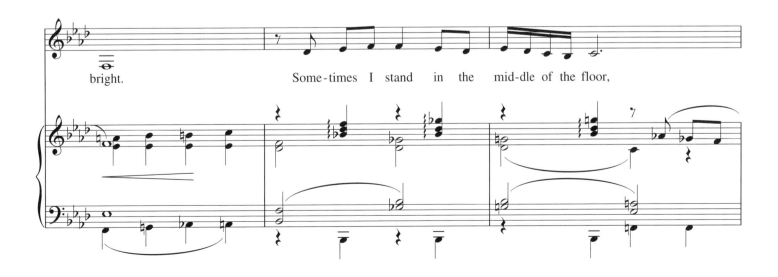

bright. Some-times I stand in the mid-dle of the floor,

ADELAIDE'S LAMENT
from *Guys And Dolls*

By FRANK LOESSER

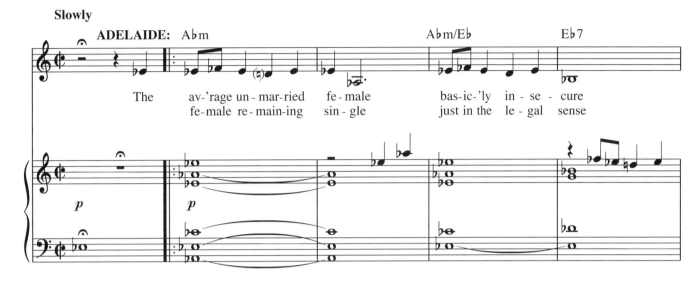

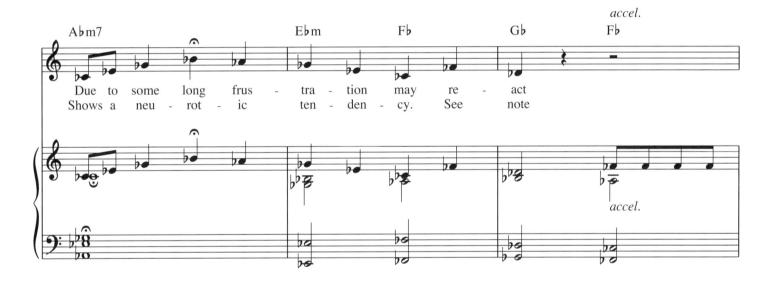

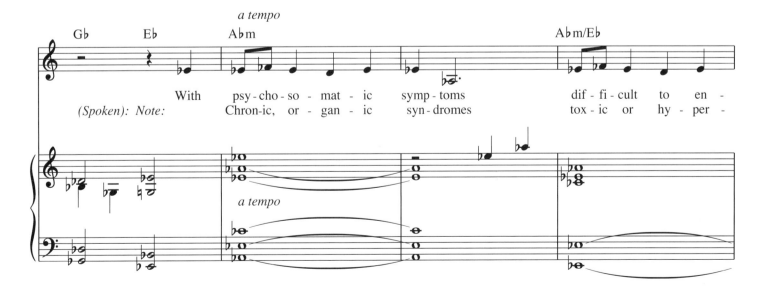

I CAN HEAR THE BELLS

from *Hairspray*

Music by MARC SHAIMAN
Lyrics by MARC SHAIMAN and SCOTT WITTMAN

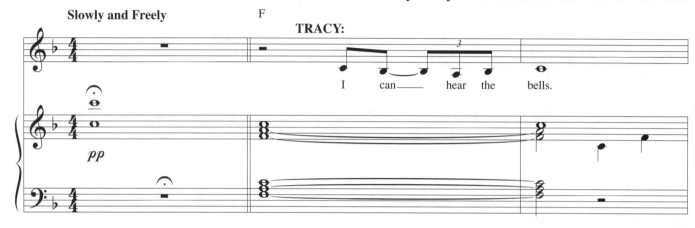

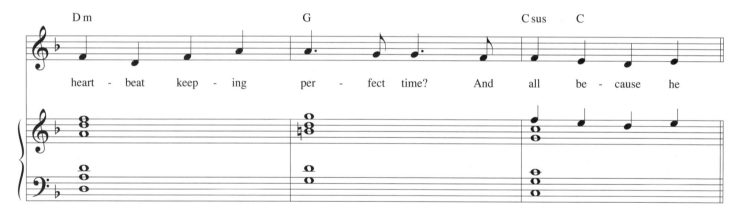

* Optional ending

I KNOW THINGS NOW

from *Into The Woods*

Words and Music by
STEPHEN SONDHEIM

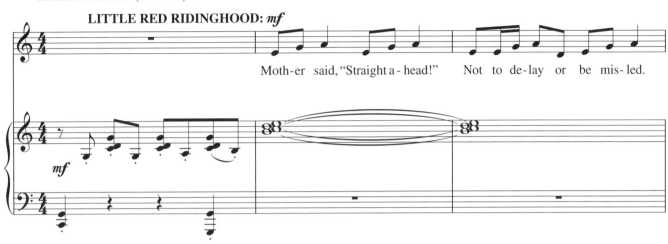

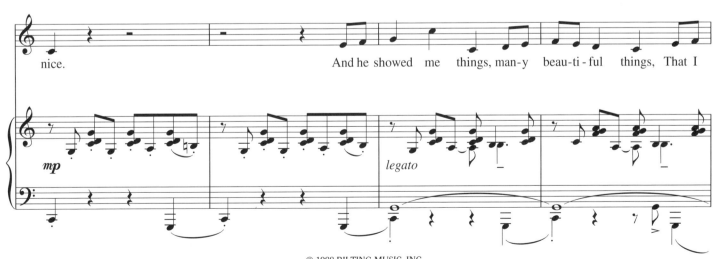

way that they should. And take ex-tra care with stran-gers, E-ven flow-ers have their dan-gers. And though

scar-y is ex-cit-ing, Nice is dif-f'rent than good.

Now I know: don't be scared. Gran-ny is right, just be pre-pared. Is-n't it nice to know a lot!

And a lit-tle bit not...

SOMEONE LIKE YOU

from the Broadway Musical *Jekyll & Hyde*

Words by LESLIE BRICUSSE
Music by FRANK WILDHORN

STILL HURTING

from *The Last Five Years*

Music and Lyrics by
JASON ROBERT BROWN

PART OF YOUR WORLD

from Walt Disney's *The Little Mermaid - A Broadway Musical*

Music by ALAN MENKEN
Lyrics by HOWARD ASHMAN

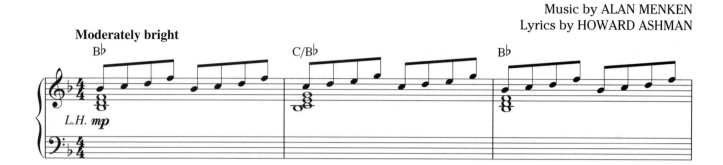

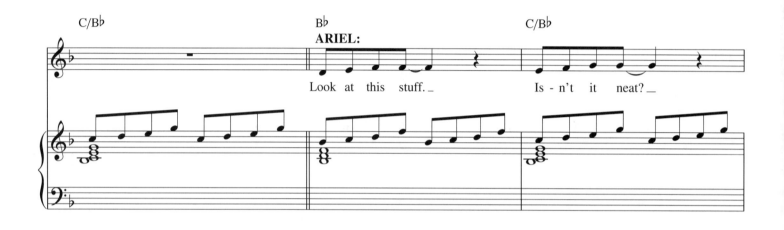

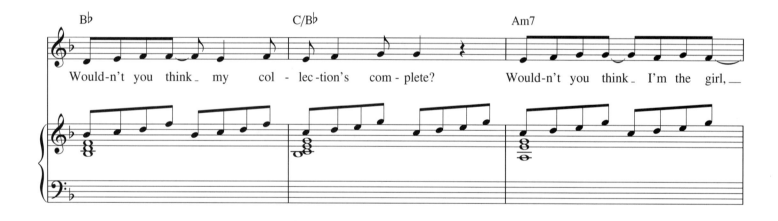

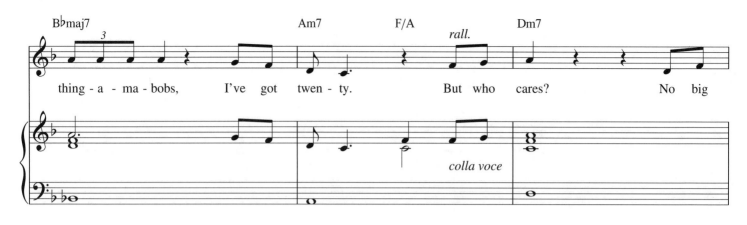

thing - a - ma - bobs, I've got twen - ty. But who cares? No big

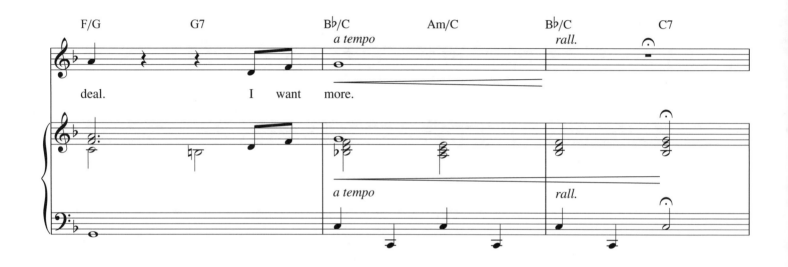

deal. I want more.

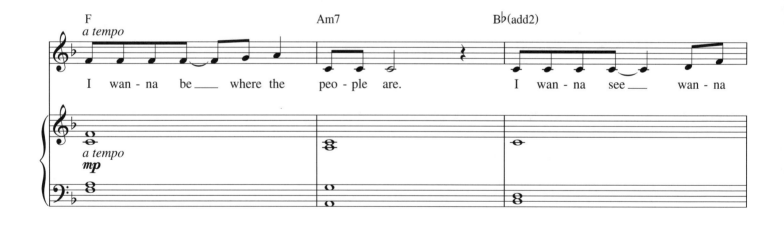

I wan - na be ___ where the peo - ple are. I wan - na see ___ wan - na

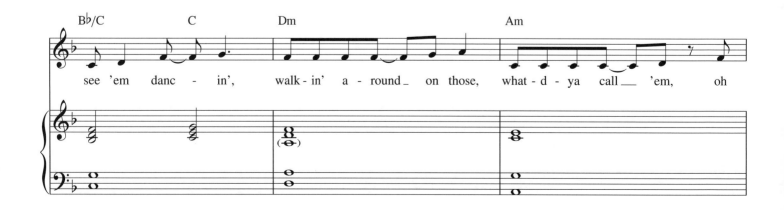

see 'em danc - in', walk - in' a - round ___ on those, what - d - ya call ___ 'em, oh

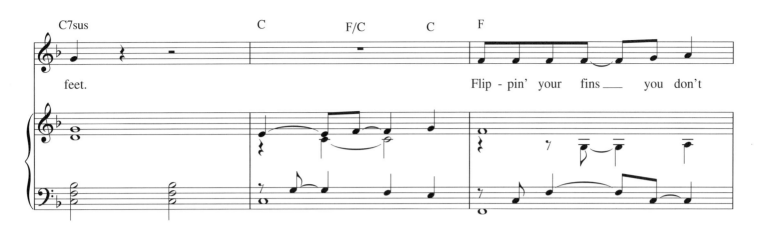

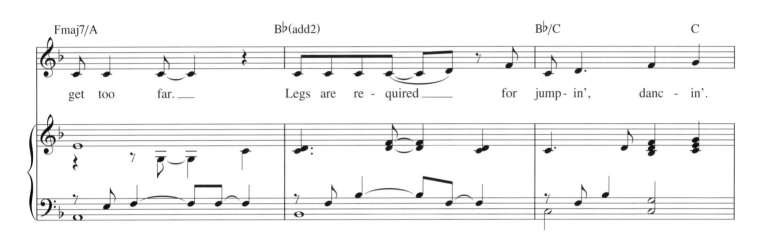

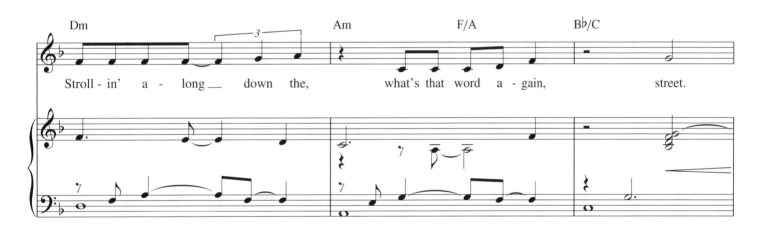

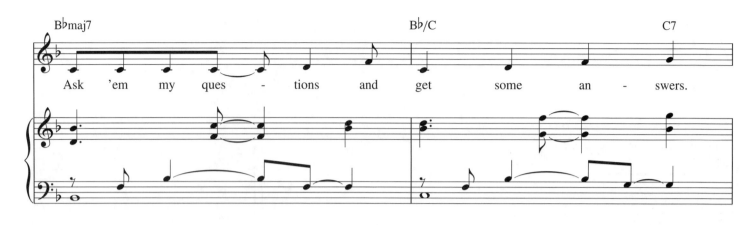

Ask 'em my ques - tions and get some an - swers.

What's a fire, _____ and why does it, what's the word,

burn. When's it my turn? Would - n't I

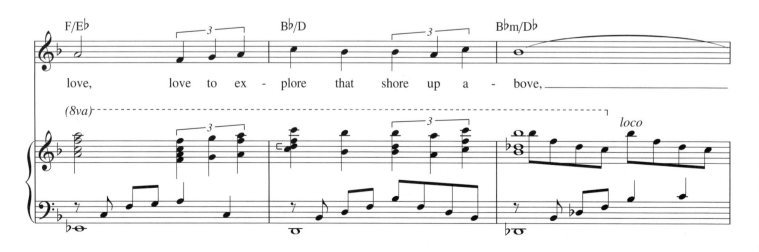

love, love to ex - plore that shore up a - bove, _____

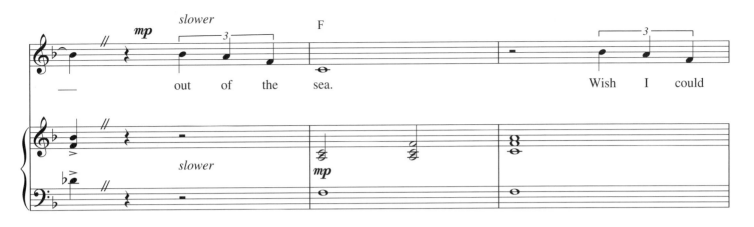

out of the sea. Wish I could

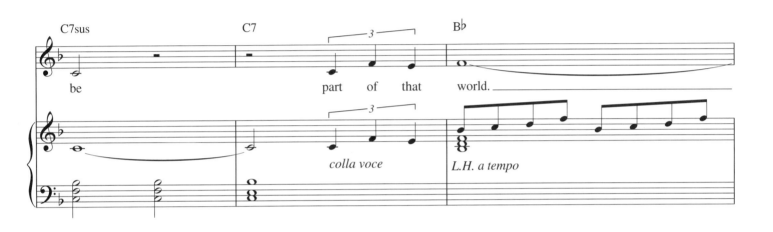

be part of that world.

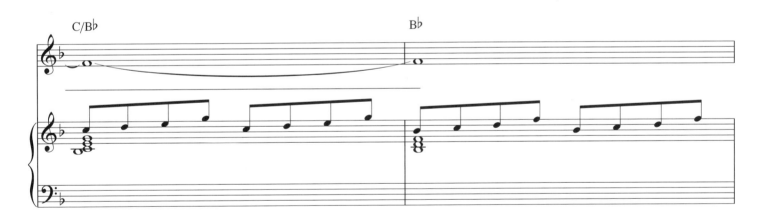

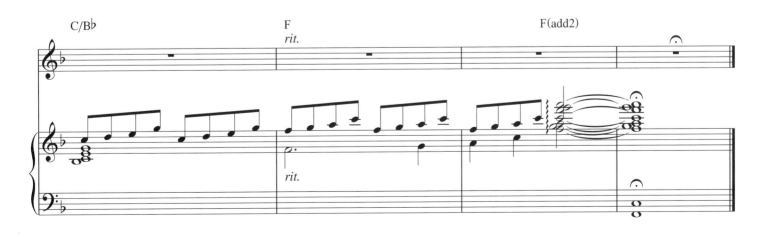

SEND IN THE CLOWNS
from the Musical *A Little Night Music*

Words and Music by
STEPHEN SONDHEIM

lines, No one is there. Don't you love

farce? My fault, I fear. I thought that you'd want what I want—Sor- ry, my

dear. But where are the clowns? Quick, send in the

clowns. Don't both- er, they're here.

THE WINNER TAKES IT ALL
from *Mamma Mia!*

Words and Music by BENNY ANDERSSON
and BJÖRN ULVAEUS

*Because the song is rather long as a solo, a possible cut could be taken to **.

I DREAMED A DREAM

from *Les Misérables*

Original French Lyrics by ALAIN BOUBLIL
and JEAN-MARC NATEL
English Lyrics by HERBERT KRETZMER
Music by CLAUDE-MICHEL SCHÖNBERG

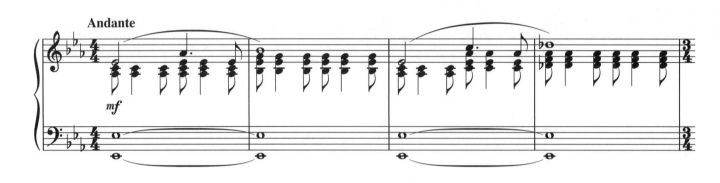

There was a time when men were kind, When their voic-es were soft

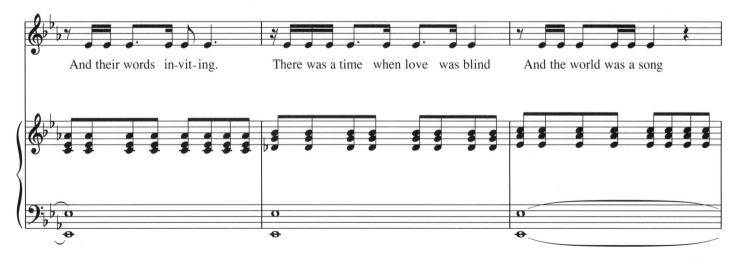

And their words in-vit-ing. There was a time when love was blind And the world was a song

And the song was ex-cit-ing. There was a time. Then it all went wrong.

Andante

FANTINE:

I dreamed a dream in time gone by When hope was high and life worth

liv-ing, I dreamed that love would nev-er die,

I dreamed that God would be for-giv-ing. Then I was young and un-af-raid And dreams were made and used and wast-ed. There was no ran-som to be paid, No song un-sung, no wine un-tast-ed.

Poco più mosso

But the ti-gers come at night

With their voi - ces soft as thun - der, As they tear your hope a -

part, As they turn your dream to shame. _____

rall. *a tempo*

He slept a sum - mer by my

rall. *p a tempo*

side, He filled my days with end - less won - der,

I CAIN'T SAY NO

from *Oklahoma!*

Lyrics by OSCAR HAMMERSTEIN II
Music by RICHARD RODGERS

It ain't so much a ques-tion of not know-in' whut to do, I

knowed whut's right and wrong since I been ten. I

heared a lot of sto-ries and I reck-on they are true A-

bout how girls 're put up - on by men. I

know I mus-n't fall in - to the pit, _____ But when I'm with a fel - ler, I fer -

git!

I'm jist a girl who cain't say no,
I'm jist a girl who cain't say no,

I cain't be pris - sy and quaint _____
In a som - bre - ro and chaps _____

I ain't the type that c'n faint _____
Soon as I sit on their laps _____

How c'n I be whut I ain't? _____ I
Sump - 'n in - side o' me snaps! _____ I

cain't _____ say _____
cain't _____ say _____

sweet - er 'n cream and he's got - ta have cream or

die? Whut you goin' to do when he

talks thet way? Spit in his eye? _____

D.S. al Coda

CODA

WHEN YOU GOT IT, FLAUNT IT

from *The Producers*

Music and Lyrics by
MEL BROOKS

Ulla sings this song with a Swedish accent in the show.

WITHOUT YOU
from *Rent*

Words and Music by
JONATHAN LARSON

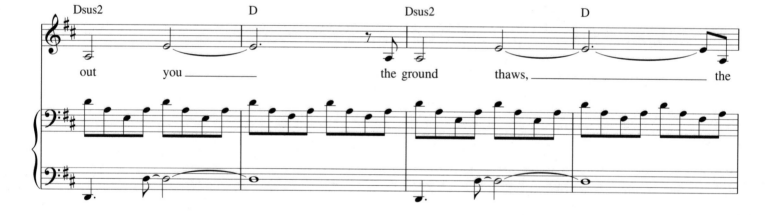

This song for Mimi and Roger has been adapted as a solo for this edition.

HONEY BUN

from *South Pacific*

Lyrics by OSCAR HAMMERSTEIN II
Music by RICHARD RODGERS

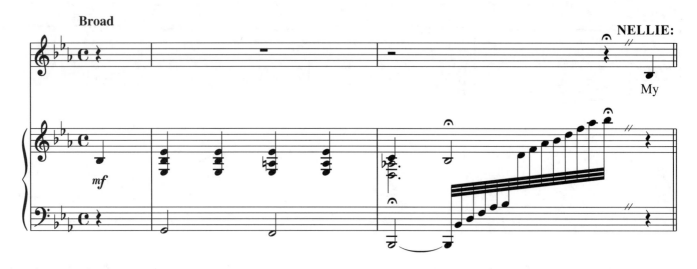

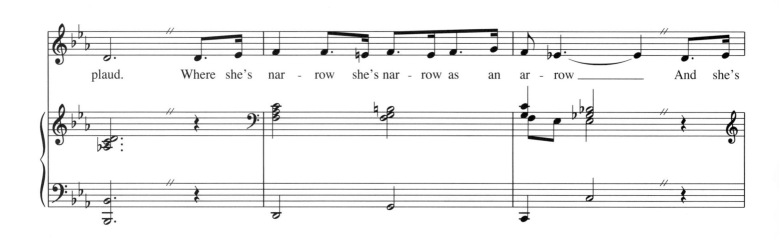

IF MY FRIENDS COULD SEE ME NOW

from *Sweet Charity*

Music by CY COLEMAN
Lyrics by DOROTHY FIELDS

Moderately bright

(spoken): The girls at the ballroom would never believe me in a million years.

CHARITY:

If they could

set up, ho - ly cow!

They'd nev-er be - lieve it!

They'd nev-er be - lieve it! If my friends could see

me now!

STARS AND THE MOON
from *Songs For A New World*

Music and Lyrics by
JASON ROBERT BROWN

Folk Rock, gentle (♩ = 60)

I met a man with-out a dol-lar to his name,___ who___ had no

traits of an-y val-ue but his smile

I met a man who had a for-tune in the bank who had re-

tired at age thir-ty set for life

I met a man and did-n't know which stars to thank and then he

asked one day if I would be his wife

GIMME GIMME
from *Thoroughly Modern Millie*

Music by JEANINE TESORI
Lyrics by DICK SCANLAN

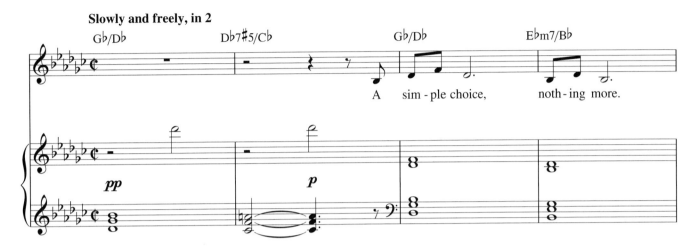

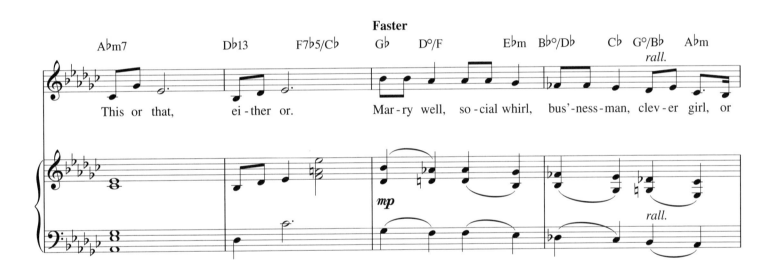

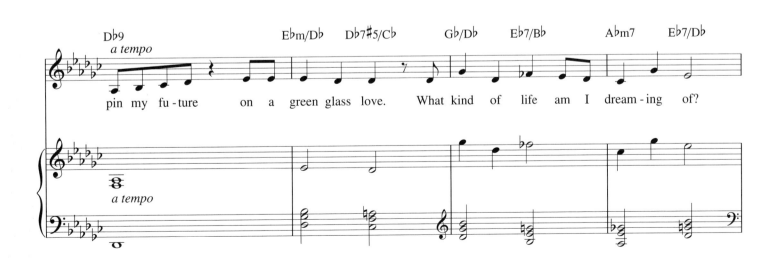

E7 A7 D9 G6
fa - mous ar - row. Gim-me gim-me that thing called love.
Faster
G♯7 G7 G♯7 C♯m
I don't care if he's a no -
cresc.
f
B♭7 A7 B♭7 E♭m
bod - y. In my heart he'll be a some -
B/D♯ D7
bod - y, some - bod - y to love

DEFYING GRAVITY
from the Broadway Musical *Wicked*

Music and Lyrics by
STEPHEN SCHWARTZ

HOW DID WE COME TO THIS?

from *The Wild Party*

Words and Music by
ANDREW LIPPA

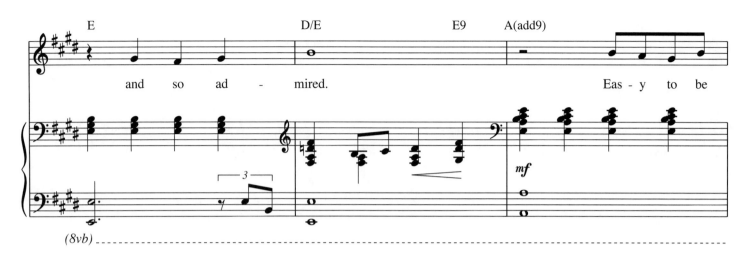

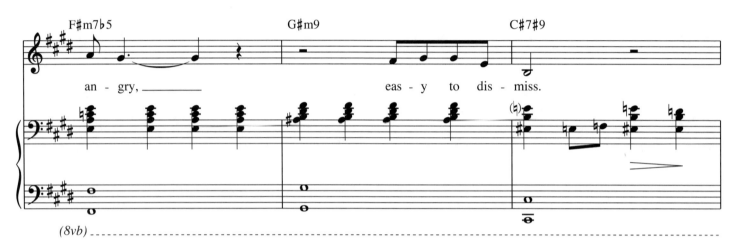

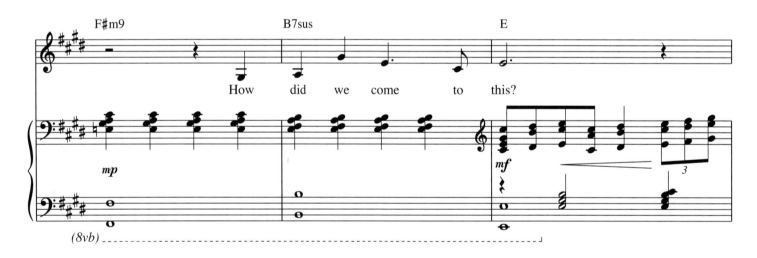